Adapted from the original by

CHARLES DICKENS

A GUINEA PIG
CHRISTMAS CAROL

BLOOMSBURY PUBLISHING
LONDON · OXFORD · NEW YORK · NEW DELHI · SYDNEY

It was Christmas Eve, and Mr Ebenezer Scrooge sat busy in his counting house, solitary as an oyster.

His business partner Marley had died seven years ago this very night, leaving the old miser to run the counting house by himself.

Nobody ever asked, "My dear Scrooge, how are you?"
But what did Scrooge care? He liked being left alone.

The door of Scrooge's office was open that he might keep his eye upon his clerk, Bob Cratchit, who sat in a dismal little cell beyond, copying letters.

Scrooge had a small fire, but the clerk's fire was so very much smaller that it looked like one coal. He couldn't make it any bigger because Scrooge kept the coal-box in his own room.

Bob tried to warm himself at the candle, but being a man of little imagination, he failed.

Just then, in came Scrooge's nephew, Fred.

"Merry Christmas, Uncle!" he said. "Will you come and dine with us on Christmas Day?"

"Christmas?" said Scrooge. "Bah! Humbug!"

The frost and fog hung about the city as Scrooge made his way home at the end of the day. But when he put his key in the lock, he glanced up at the door knocker, and saw that it was no longer a brass knocker…

…it had transformed into Marley's face!

And then it was a knocker again. "Pooh pooh!" thought Scrooge, closing the door with a bang.

Up Scrooge went to bed, not caring a button for the dark: darkness is cheap, and Scrooge liked it.

But then he heard the sound of a heavy chain being dragged up the stairs and coming straight towards his door.

It was Marley's Ghost!

"I am here tonight to warn you," said the Ghost, "that you have yet a chance and hope of escaping my own sad fate. You will be haunted by Three Spirits of Christmas. Expect the first tomorrow, when the clock strikes one."

Scrooge tried saying "Humbug!"
but stopped at the first syllable.

BONG... THE HOUR BELL

OUNDED, A DEEP, DULL, HOLLOW, MELANCHOLY ONE

Scrooge found himself face to face with the First Spirit.

It wore a tunic of the purest white; and round its waist was bound a lustrous belt, the sheen of which was beautiful to behold.

"Who, and what are you?" Scrooge demanded.

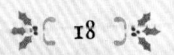

"I am the Ghost of Christmas Past."

They passed through a wall and travelled back in time and across open fields until they came to the village where Scrooge had grown up.

☆

The Spirit pointed to a building of dull red brick. "The school is not quite deserted," said the Spirit. "A solitary child, neglected by his friends, is left there still."

It was Scrooge when he had been a small
lonely schoolboy on Christmas Day.

"Poor boy!" said Scrooge. "Spirit, show me no more!"

"I told you these were the shadows of things that have been," said the Spirit. "That they are what they are, do not blame me!"

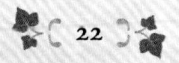

And then Scrooge found himself in his bedroom
again, where he sank into a heavy sleep.

BONG!

BONG! ... THE CLOCK STRUCK THE HOUR OF TWO

Scrooge awoke to see his own room, but it had undergone a surprising transformation. There was holly and mistletoe everywhere, and a mighty blaze in the fireplace.

In the middle of the room stood a jolly Giant, glorious to see.

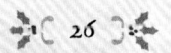

"I am the Ghost of Christmas Present!"

The good Spirit led Scrooge straight to Bob Cratchit's house. At the table sat Mrs Cratchit, waiting to carve a very small turkey.

Then in came Bob Cratchit, with his son Tiny Tim upon his shoulder. Alas for Tiny Tim, he bore a little crutch.

Bob took up his place at the table and proposed a toast. "A Merry Christmas to us all, my dears!"

"God bless us, every one!" said Tiny Tim.

"Tiny Tim looks so frail, Spirit," said Scrooge.
"Tell me if he will live?"

"I see a vacant seat," replied the Spirit, "and a crutch without an owner. If these shadows remain unaltered by the future, the child will die."

"Oh no," said Scrooge. "Oh no, kind Spirit! Say he will be spared."

Then he heard Bob making another toast.

"I give you Mr Scrooge," declared Bob, "the Founder of the Feast!"

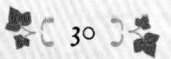

"Founder of the Feast indeed!" said Mrs Cratchit.
"That odious, stingy, hard, unfeeling man!"

By this time it was getting dark, and snowing pretty heavily. Scrooge and the Spirit continued through the streets until they reached the house of Scrooge's nephew.

"... and my uncle said that Christmas was a humbug!" Fred declared to his guests. "Still, I mean to invite him to dine with us every year, whether he likes it or not. Here is a glass of mulled wine to hand – let us toast, to Uncle Scrooge!"

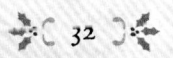

"A Merry Christmas and a Happy New Year
to the old man, wherever he is!"

BONG... TH

LOCK STRUCK AGAIN, BONG! ... BONG!

Scrooge looked about him for the jolly Giant,
but it had vanished.

Then he beheld a solemn phantom, draped and hooded,
coming like a mist along the ground towards him.

"Am I in the presence of the Ghost of Christmas
Yet To Come?" asked Scrooge.

The Spirit answered not, but pointed onward.

The Spirit and Scrooge walked through the city. The Spirit stopped beside a little knot of men.

Scrooge knew these men. They were men of business: very wealthy, and of great importance. They were talking of an acquaintance who had recently died.

"When did he die?" asked one man.

"Last night, I believe," his friend replied.

"It's likely to be a very cheap funeral," the first man said. "I don't know of anybody to go to it."

"Spirit, I feel our parting moment is at hand," said Scrooge. "Tell me, who is the man who has died?"

The Spirit led him to a churchyard and stood among the graves, pointing down to one. Scrooge crept towards it, trembling as he went, and following the Spirit's finger, read upon the stone his own name.

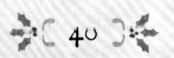

"Spirit! Help me to avoid this lonely fate!" cried Scrooge. "I am not the man I was. I will honour Christmas in my heart, and try to keep it all the year."

"I will live in the Past, the Present, and the Future!
The Spirits of all Three shall live within me!"

DING, DONG, BELL – THE

CHRISTMAS BELLS RANG OUT... BELL, DONG, DING!

Scrooge awoke, and he was home. The bed was his own, the room was his own. Best and happiest of all, the Time before him was his own, to make amends in!

He rushed into the street. Golden sunlight; Heavenly sky; sweet fresh air; merry bells. Oh, glorious. Glorious!

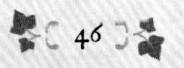

"I am as giddy as a schoolboy! A Merry Christmas to everybody! A Happy New Year to all the world!"

"What's the day today?" cried Scrooge to a passing boy.

"Today!" replied the boy. "Why, CHRISTMAS DAY!"

"Do you know if the Poulterer's have sold the prize Turkey?"

"The one as big as me?" replied the boy. "No, it's sitting there now."

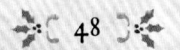

"We'll send it to Bob Cratchit!" said Scrooge.

When Bob Cratchit came into the office, Scrooge declared "Merry Christmas, Bob! I have decided to raise your salary and help Tiny Tim!"

"Here," said Scrooge, "have a cup of mulled wine!"

Scrooge walked about the streets, and watched the people excitedly hurrying to and fro with presents, and patted children on the head. He had never dreamed that any walk – that anything – could give him so much pleasure.

☆

Finally, he turned his steps towards his nephew's house. "Why bless my soul," said Fred when he heard the knock upon the door. "Who's that?"

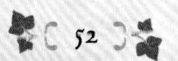

"It's I, your uncle Scrooge, come to dinner.
Will you let me in, Fred?"

And henceforth it was always said of Scrooge,
that he knew how to keep Christmas well. To Tiny Tim,
who did NOT die, he was a second father.

And so, as Tiny Tim observed, *God bless Us, Every One!*

THE END

OSCAR

BEVERLIE-ANNE

BEAR

SUPER HANS

ELSIE

MINTY

GRACIE

CHOCOLATE

DOLLY

DORIS

MARLIN

MABEL

SHERLOCK

CHARACTERS & CAST

Charles Dickens . . . . OSCAR

Ebenezer Scrooge . . . . BEVERLIE-ANNE

Scrooge as a Schoolboy . . . . BEAR

Fred, Scrooge's Nephew . . . . SUPER HANS

Bob Cratchit . . . . ELSIE

Tiny Tim Cratchit . . . . MINTY

Mrs Cratchit . . . . GRACIE

First Businessman . . . . CHOCOLATE

Second Businessman . . . . DOLLY

Marley's Ghost . . . . DORIS

Ghost of Christmas Past . . . . MARLIN

Ghost of Christmas Present . . . . MABEL

Ghost of Christmas Yet To Come . . . . SHERLOCK

The publishers would like to thank Pauline, Amanda, Izzy, Jen, Si, Rebecca, Sophia, Oliver and *ohmyguinea*'s Becky, as well as Charles, Rosie, Barbara, Elizabeth, Jack and our other friends for making every photography shoot feel like Christmas. Thanks also to that most affable carpenter, Alfred.

A particular thank you to photographer and designer Phillip Beresford for his remarkable skilfulness and for always making us (and the guinea pigs) smile.

CHARLES DICKENS was born in 1812 and he has gone down in history as one of the most well-loved novelists in English literature. His book *A Christmas Carol* was an instant bestseller when it was published in December 1843 and the first edition sold out, appropriately enough, on Christmas Eve.

TESS NEWALL was born in 1987 and when she is not sprinkling snow on the streets of Victorian London or making guinea-pig-sized spectacles she works as a freelance set designer, specializing in fashion shoots, window displays and decorative interiors. She lives in London.

ALEX GOODWIN was born in 1985 and he has an MA in Creative Writing from the University of East Anglia. Some people have noticed that much of his writing comes to the length of a medium-sized shopping list; this is explained by the fact that a picture of a guinea pig says a thousand words. He lives in London.

Small pets are abandoned every day, but the lucky ones end up in rescue centres where they can be looked after and rehomed. You may not know it, but some of these centres are devoted entirely to guinea pigs. They work with welfare organizations to give first class advice and information, as well as finding happy new homes for the animals they look after. If Scrooge's transformation makes you feel all warm and cosy inside, perhaps you'll share the festive spirit by supporting your local rescue centre!

BLOOMSBURY PUBLISHING
Bloomsbury Publishing Plc
50 Bedford Square, London, WC1B 3DP, UK

BLOOMSBURY, BLOOMSBURY PUBLISHING and the Diana logo are trademarks of Bloomsbury Publishing Plc

First published in Great Britain 2018

A catalogue record for this book is available from the British Library

Library of Congress Cataloguing-in-Publication data has been applied for

ISBN UK: HB: 978-1-5266-0145-2
ISBN U.S. : HB: 978-1-63557-311-4

2 4 6 8 10 9 7 5 3 1

Costumes and props by Tess Newall
Photography and design by Phillip Beresford
Abridgement by Alex Goodwin
Edited by Xa Shaw Stewart

Printed and bound in China by C&C Offset Printing Co., Ltd

All papers used by Bloomsbury Publishing Plc are natural, recyclable products made from wood grown in well-managed forests. Our manufacturing processes conform to the environmental regulations of the country of origin